THE
Shoemaker
AND THE ELVES

RETOLD BY RUTH MATTISON • ILLUSTRATIONS BY OLGA ZAKHAROVA

PIONEER VALLEY EDUCATIONAL PRESS, INC.

Once upon a time a shoemaker
and his wife lived in
a little house over a shoe shop.
They were very, very poor.

One day, the shoemaker
said to his wife,
"Here is some leather.
I can make just one more
pair of shoes with this leather.
We have no money
to buy more."

The shoemaker cut the leather.
"I will make the shoes
tomorrow," he said.
"Let's go to bed."

The next morning, the shoemaker woke up and went into his shop. The leather was gone.
On the table was a pair of beautiful shoes.

"Come here!" called the shoemaker to his wife. "Look at the shoes!"

The shoemaker's wife went
into the shop. "Oh, my," she said.
"They are beautiful shoes!
Did you make them?"

"No!" said the shoemaker.

"Then who did?" asked his wife.

"I don't know," said the shoemaker.

The shoemaker's wife put the shoes
in the shop window.

A woman stopped and looked
at the shoes.
"Oh, what beautiful shoes,"
said the woman, and she went
into the shop to buy them.

"Now I can buy leather to make two pairs of shoes!"
said the shoemaker.

The shoemaker cut the leather
and went to bed.

The next morning, the shoemaker
went into his shop. The leather
was gone. On the table
were two pairs of beautiful shoes.

The shoemaker's wife
put the two pairs of shoes
in the shop window.

A man came into the shop
to buy a pair of shoes.

Then another man
came into the shop
to buy the second pair of shoes.

"Now I can buy leather
to make four pairs of shoes!"
said the shoemaker.

Every night, the shoemaker cut the leather. Every morning, he went into the shop and found new, beautiful shoes.

Everyone wanted a pair of the shoes.

"We must find out who is making the shoes," said the shoemaker's wife.

COUNTRY MOUSE and a TOWN MOUSE

Retold by Ruth Mattison • Illustrated by Max Stasuyk

A Country Mouse and A Town Mouse
ISBN 978-1-58453-552-2
ISBN 978-1-58453-555-3 (Set of 6 titles)
Retold by Ruth Mattison
Illustrated by Max Stasuyk
Book Design by Heather Rush & Karen Woodward

Printed in the United States of America.

10 9 8 7 6 5 4 3 2

That night, the shoemaker
and his wife stayed up
and hid behind a door.
At midnight, two little elves
came into the shop. They sat down
and began to work. They worked
and worked. The elves
made all the leather into shoes.

"The little elves have done so much for us. I am going to make new clothes for them," said the shoemaker's wife.

"I will make them some shoes," said the shoemaker.

The next night, the little elves came in and saw the new clothes and shoes. They put them on and began to dance around. Then they danced out of the shop. The shoemaker and his wife never saw the elves again, but after that they always had good luck.

Dear Elves,
thank you for
all your help!